QUARTERBACK SEASON

FRED BOWEN
SPORTS STORY *series*

FRED BOWEN series
SPORTS STORY

QUARTERBACK SEASON

FRED BOWEN

PEACHTREE
ATLANTA

Published by
PEACHTREE PUBLISHERS
1700 Chattahoochee Avenue
Atlanta, Georgia 30318-2112
www.peachtree-online.com

Text © 2011 by Fred Bowen

Cover design by Thomas Gonzalez and Maureen Withee
Book design by Melanie McMahon Ives

Printed in April 2013 in Harrisonburg, VA, by R.R. Donnelley & Sons
United States of America
10 9 8 7 6 5 4 3

Library of Congress Cataloging-in-Publication Data
    Bowen, Fred.
        Quarterback season / written by Fred Bowen.
            p. cm.
        Summary: As a school assignment, eighth-grader Matt Monroe keeps a journal about his team's football season.
        ISBN 978-1-56145-594-2 / 1-56145-594-6
        [1. Football--Fiction. 2. Diaries--Fiction.] I. Title.

    PZ7.B6724Qu 2011
    [Fic]--dc22

                                                    2011002673

To the memory of my father,
Thomas J. Bowen,
who taught me to appreciate good writing.

Tuesday

First day of school. Im glad I'm finaly in 8th grade bc its fun being in the oldest class at Parkside middle. But I can't believe it. We already have homework in english class. We have to keep a journal. 3 entries a week. For the whole semester! I don't even like writing thank you notes to my grandparents. Now I have to write something 3 times a week and im not even getting a gift.

Okay, thats my first entry.

Wednesday

After school today I went to North Park to practice throwing passes to my best freind, Brandon Gonzalez. Tryouts for the

Parkside football team are next week! Im sure Coach Mack is going to pick me to be the starting QB bc I was the backup last year. Brandon will definately start at wide receiver. We are totally pumped about football!!!

Friday

I dont know what I should write about today. Nothing really happened except my dog Elway threw up on my dads shoes this morning and my dad yelled at me for giving Elway mashed potatos last night at dinner. How could I know the potatos were going to come out of the wrong end?

OK, that's 3 entries.

From: Ignacio.S@ParksideMS.WCPS.gov
Date: Sunday, September 5
To: MattQB7@Monroe37family.com

Matt—

Get serious! You can do so much better than this. Your journal entries are much too short and have several careless errors, including misspelled words. You will be marked down for both. Each entry should be at least two paragraphs. Next time, include the dates, don't take shortcuts, and pay more attention to spellcheck! It also wouldn't hurt to check over your entries before you send them.

I can tell that you love football because you talk about it with such enthusiasm. I think football is a great subject for your journal. Why don't you begin with tryouts and then describe the season as it goes along?

If you can talk about football with enthusiasm, you can write about football with enthusiasm.

Ms. Samantha Ignacio
English Department
Parkside Middle School

Write what makes you happy.
            —O. Henry

Tuesday 9/7

Paragraph 1.

Okay, my journal can be all about football. That should be more fun than writing thank you notes, but it's still writing. It will be all about football, but without the misspellings and stuff. (Really, Ms. Ig.)

Paragraph 2.

Today was the first day of tryouts. Coach Mack made everybody run a mile around the track and timed us. I came in seventh out of fifty kids. That's pretty good. Brandon was better. He came in second. That's okay, though. He *should* be faster than me. He's a wide receiver. The fastest kid on the team was a seventh grader named Devro. Some kids think he might be the starting quarterback this season. Give me a break! If he's so fast, he should be a running back or a wide receiver. Or run really fast to some other school that needs a quarterback.

Wednesday 9/8
Paragraph 1.

Second day of tryouts. Coach Mack says nobody is going to get cut from the team, so we're just trying out for positions. Lots of kids want to be the quarterback, but most of them stink. Some of those guys couldn't throw a wad of paper into a recycling bin if they were standing right next to it.

Paragraph 2.

I was awesome during quarterback drills. I hit all the receivers right in the hands, even on the long fly patterns. Coach decided to keep four players at quarterback. Of course, I'm one of them. Two others—

Andre Wilson and Russell Parker—are eighth graders like me. The last one is that new kid, Devro. I'm not worried. I can beat out all those guys.

Thursday 9/9
Paragraph 1.

We had practice again today. We did a bunch of exercises and stuff.

Paragraph 2.

Coach still hasn't decided who's going to be the starting quarterback. Devro is getting annoying. He's always clapping his hands and trying to pump everybody up. He acts likes he's already the starting quarterback. Maybe he doesn't understand that I'm going to be the starting QB.

From: Ignacio.S@ParksideMS.WCPS.gov
Date: Thursday, September 9
To: MattQB7@Monroe37family.com

Matt—

You are a very good student; your journal should be much better. Remember, the journal is an important part (25%) of the first-quarter grade. I'm sure I don't need to remind you that you can't play football unless you pass all your subjects.

Please rewrite your journal entries for the first two days of tryouts and send them to me tomorrow. Please include more details this time. Keep in mind that I am not a football fan. You'll need to explain football terms such as "fly pattern."

I told you earlier that journal entries must be at least two paragraphs, but I expect a good student like you to write more. Do not number your paragraphs and please spell out the date of each entry.

Talk to me after class if you have any questions.

Ms. Samantha Ignacio
English Department
Parkside Middle School

The best writing is rewriting.
—E. B. White

Tuesday, September 7 (AGAIN!)

Football tryouts have started and Coach Mack is working us hard.

First, he made everybody run a mile—that's four laps around the track—and timed us. The mile wasn't that tough because we were wearing sweatpants and T-shirts, not full football gear. Brandon and I have been running all summer. My buddy, Colby Johnson, has been running with us too. So we were ready. Colby is our best offensive lineman, but he's not as fast as Brandon or me.

Our times for the mile were:
Brandon—5:54 (5 minutes and 54 seconds)
Me (Matt)—6:15
Colby—6:58

I came in seventh out of fifty kids trying out. Brandon came in second and Colby finished in the middle of the pack. The kid who came in first is some seventh grader named Devro Beech. He's really fast. And really annoying.

Next, Coach made us do a bunch of calisthenics—jumping jacks, push-ups, toe touches, and all sorts of sprints. We were sweating like pigs. The hardest things were the leg lifts. They were brutal. We had to lift our legs up, spread them, put them back together, and then let them down slowly. Leg lifts are supposed to toughen up your stomach muscles, but I thought my legs were going to fall off.

Wednesday, September 8 (AGAIN!)

During practice today Coach let us go to the positions we wanted to play. Lots of kids want to play quarterback. So the assistant coach, Mr. Shortall, had us take a hike from center, drop back, and throw passes to receivers who were running patterns.

Some of the kids were pathetic. They couldn't throw the ball more than 15 yards. The other kids were teasing them, saying they threw like girls...or worse, like linemen. No way they'll get to play quarterback.

After all my practice with Brandon, I was awesome. I hit all the receivers right in the hands, even on the long fly patterns. (Ms. Ig: That's when the receiver runs straight downfield, about 25 yards or more.) After everybody threw a bunch of passes, Coach Shortall chose four guys to keep at quarterback—me, two other eighth graders, Andre Wilson and Russell Parker, and that seventh-grade kid, Devro.

Later, Coach Shortall told Andre Wilson the team needed him to play defense. Yeah, right. He just wasn't very good at quarterback.

So now there are just three of us. I'm not that worried about Russell and I don't worry about seventh graders. And, like I said, Devro is a seventh grader.

From: Ignacio.S@ParksideMS.WCPS.gov
Date: Sunday, September 12
To: MattQB7@Monroe37family.com

Matt—

   Your revisions were much better. The details you included gave me a clearer picture of what it is like to be at practice and part of the team.

   You say you are certain you will be the starting quarterback and that Devro is not a threat to you. Is that what you are really thinking? Try to be honest about your feelings.

   Keep up the good work. And remember to include a lot of interesting details in your writing.

Ms. Samantha Ignacio
English Department
Parkside Middle School

I write in order to understand what I am thinking.
—Abraham Verghese

Monday, September 13

The coaches handed out equipment today—football pants, shoulder pads, helmets, and shirts. We'll be working out in full pads from now on.

During practice, the coaches gave Devro and me the same number of reps, or repetitions. (That's football talk for turns running the plays.) I can't believe they are giving Devro so many reps at quarterback. So now he probably thinks he's going to be the starting quarterback.

After practice, the coaches gave a playbook to every player. It's a blue three-ring binder with about forty diagrammed plays in it. I wrote "Quarterbacks Rule" on the front of mine with a marker. (How's that for details, Ms. Ig?)

I already know about 90% of the plays from last year.

I watched Devro when he opened his playbook and saw all those complicated diagrams. He started looking really hard at one of them, but I don't think he understood it. In fact, he looked like he was going to be sick to his stomach.

That made me feel better. (Those are my honest feelings, Ms. Ig.) Knowing the plays will be a BIG advantage for me.

The coaches also handed out our schedule.

PARKSIDE MIDDLE SCHOOL
FOOTBALL SCHEDULE

9/23	CHURCHILL MS	3 pm
9/30	at WESTERN MS	3 pm
10/7	BEVERLY MS	3 pm
10/14	at BULLIS SCHOOL	3 pm
10/21	FALLS ROAD MS	3 pm
10/28	ROBERT FROST MS	3 pm
11/4	at RENWICH MS	3:30 pm
11/11	at LAMPETER MS	3 pm
11/18	CHAMPIONSHIP GAME	TBA

The top two teams play in a championship game at the end of the year. That's what we're aiming for, the championship game.

Wednesday, September 15

One of the things I love about football is the plays. There are lots of cool signals and secret codes to football plays. Here's the passing tree from our playbook. It should explain the pass patterns.

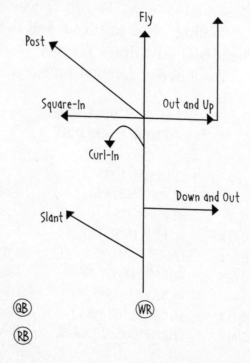

We spent most of the last two practices running simple plays like 35-Dive over and over again. That's when the quarterback (me) turns to his left and hands the ball to the running back, who then takes off with Colby, our left tackle and best offensive lineman, blocking for him all the way.

Coach had us run 36-Dive a lot too. That's when the running back heads toward the right. After a while, though, I got bored just handing the ball off to Jordan Jenkins, our best running back. But Coach Mack said he wanted us to know those plays for our scrimmage next Monday and for the first game against Churchill.

I'm always glad when we get to the pass plays. That's my absolute favorite part of practice. I love to throw the football and watch it flying through the air in a tight spiral.

Devro is having trouble with the plays. I'll bet his head is spinning from all the signals and numbers and stuff. Sometimes he gets the moves all wrong. Like today, Devro turned to his right to hand the ball off to

Jordan on the 35-Dive play. The only problem? Jordan was going to his left. Devro just stood there with the ball, looking like a dope.

Coach Mack yelled at Devro and then pointed to me, "Matt, get in there and show Devro how to run a 35-Dive." Listening to Coach yelling at him, I almost felt sorry for Devro.

But not really. (Another honest feeling, Ms. Ig!)

Friday, September 17

This big eighth grader named Dan Jankowski quit today. Everyone thought he was going to start as a lineman on offense. But he told Coach Mack he didn't want to play football. Colby said we won't miss him because he's nothing but a wimp who likes to sit around and play video games. I guess Dan would rather play football with his thumbs on a remote control. Too bad. All you get doing that is strong thumbs.

Still, it felt funny watching Dan walk away in his regular clothes while the rest of us were in our football stuff. In a way it was like he was telling us that playing football was stupid.

To tell you the truth, I can't believe football is much fun for the linemen. They have to spend all their time pushing and shoving each other around in the middle of the field. They never get to throw the ball like me or run for a touchdown like Jordan or Brandon.

Colby tells me I'm wrong. He likes smacking other linemen around.

I'm glad there are guys like Colby because it's tough to have a good team without a good offensive line. When Pop-Pop (that's my grandfather), comes over to our house to watch football on TV, he always says, "Running backs are a dime a dozen. Give me a good offensive line." Pop-Pop's been watching football for almost sixty years, so I guess he knows what he's talking about.

We voted for a team manager today. The manager helps the coaches and keeps all the practice and game statistics.

We elected Michelle Campano, an eighth grader who is super smart at math. Keeping the stats should be easy for her, but I think the main reason she won is because she's real pretty. Believe me, if you have fifty boys our age voting in an election, chances are the winner is going to be a pretty girl.

Sunday, September 19

I was supposed to be doing my home-work tonight, but I was thinking about foot-ball. I know I already have three entries for this week, but I felt like writing this. (Can you believe it, Ms. Ig? I'm doing an *extra* entry. Maybe I should get *extra* credit?)

I've got to admit, I'm getting worried about Devro. To be *honest*, he's really good, especially for a seventh grader. He's the fastest runner on the team and can throw the ball pretty well. Not as well as me, but he's got a good arm.

But Devro sure acts like he's a big deal, always chest bumping guys after a good play. And whenever he makes a touchdown, he throws his arms in the air like he's some world champion. It's so annoying. Brandon says Devro just loves football. Hey, I love football, too, but I don't go around acting like that.

I've *got* to be the starting quarterback. I've been telling everybody and walking around school like I was going to be the starting quarterback.

From: Ignacio.S@ParksideMS.WCPS.gov
Date: Sunday, September 19
To: MattQB7@Monroe37family.com

Matt—

Your journal entries for last week were very good. All four of them! I liked it when you talked about the linemen. That was very interesting to me.

Thanks for the schedule (and the passing tree). Maybe I will come to a game. I live near Renwich Middle School.

I think you are hitting your stride as a writer. The most important thing is to keep your eyes open. Good writers (and good quarterbacks) are very observant. Not everything is as it seems. So pay attention and think. If you do, your journal will keep getting better and better.

Ms. Samantha Ignacio
English Department
Parkside Middle School

Any life will provide the material for writing, if it is attended to.
—Wallace Stegner

Monday, September 20

Today we played a controlled scrimmage against Woods Academy. A controlled scrimmage is different than a regular season game. The coaches for both teams are right on the field, not on the sidelines. They are supposed to talk to the players after each play to help us get better. Most of the time they just yell at us.

The good news is that Coach Mack played me at quarterback for the first series of plays. The bad news is that he played Devro just as much.

I did okay. Most of the time I handed the ball off to our starting running back, Jordan, who ran in back of our best blockers, Colby and Brady Terres (the guy who took Dan Jankowski's place). We picked up a couple of first downs that way.

I threw one pass during the first group of plays. I called Wide-Right/Curl-In. We had practiced that a million times at North Park. Brandon ran downfield about ten yards and curled toward the middle. I hit him right on the numbers and we gained about 12 yards.

Both coaches seemed happy. Coach Shortall slapped me on the top of my helmet and said, "Good job, Matt!" But on the next set of plays they put Devro in at quarterback.

He looked nervous at first. On one play he turned the wrong way and got crushed by a Woods Academy defensive lineman.

"Devro didn't look so hot on that play," Brandon whispered to me on the sidelines.

Brandon and Colby are rooting for me to beat out Devro for starting quarterback. I know we're all supposed to be "one for all" and "all for one" on the team, but the honest truth is that you want to play with your buddies.

A few plays later, Devro looked like he was caught behind the line of scrimmage for a loss. But he shook off a Woods Academy tackler and took off for a long gain. He might have gone all the way, but the Woods Academy coach blew his whistle and started yelling at his defense.

"Wow, did you see that?" Brandon asked.

"Yeah," I said.

That's why I'm worried about Devro. He's so fast and shifty that he can turn a busted play into a really big gain—or even a touchdown.

I can't do that. But I can do other stuff.

Late in the scrimmage Coach Mack called my favorite pass pattern—a Wide Right/Out and Up. I faded back and faked a Down and Out to Brandon. The Woods Academy cornerback went for the fake. Brandon turned upfield on the "up" part of the pattern and I let it fly. The ball flew in a perfect spiral right into Brandon's hands.

Touchdown! I looked over to Coach Mack and Coach Shortall. They were pumping their fists and smiling. So was I!

When Brandon came back to the huddle, I could have kissed him. Not really—that would be super weird, especially on a football field—but you know what I mean. That play might have won me the starting quarterback job.

Tuesday, September 21

All right! Coach Mack gave me most of the reps at quarterback today. It looks like he's going to make me the starter. He had Devro practicing punt and kickoff returns. I noticed that Devro wasn't strutting around as much during practice today.

They finally gave out game uniforms. We got white shirts with blue lettering, white game pants, and cool-looking silver helmets. Best of all, I got number 7. That's John Elway's old number. My dad always says Elway was the best quarterback ever. That's why he named our dog after him.

I hope I'm a better quarterback than Elway is a dog. He barfed on the living room rug last night. It was tuna casserole vomit. (I didn't think I gave him *that* much.) And then he started licking it! I guess Elway really likes tuna casserole.

(Is that too many details, Ms. Ig?)

Wednesday, September 22

Near the end of practice, Coach Mack called Devro and me to the sidelines for a talk. He said I was going to be the starting quarterback in tomorrow's game against Churchill Middle School. He wants me to play most of the downs, but he might use Devro at quarterback for some plays. Finally, he told Devro that he would be the team's kickoff and punt returner.

Devro and I just nodded. We both acted cool. But inside, I wanted to yell as loud as I could, *Yes! I am the starting quarterback for Parkside Middle School!*

Friday, September 24

I've written my three entries for this week, but I've got to write about our first game. It was awesome.

Yesterday was perfect for football, sunny but not too hot. Lots of people were in the stands, including my mom and dad. They even brought Elway.

Churchill won the coin toss and elected to receive. Our defense stopped them and they had to punt. Devro ran the punt back about 25 yards to give us good field position around the 50-yard line.

I was so excited when I ran onto the field that I had to take a couple of deep breaths to calm down. I was happy Coach Mack called some simple running plays to start us off. I was even happier when Jordan got a first down with a nice run.

We kept pounding the ball into the Churchill line until we got to the five-yard line. On second down, Coach called Fake-36/Tight End Out. I faked a handoff to Jordan and rolled out to my right. Our tight end, Luke Constantino, slipped behind the defense and was wide open in the end zone. I tossed him the ball for an easy touchdown. I had my first touchdown pass of the year!

(Note to Ms. Ig: Middle school teams don't have kickers like the pros to kick extra points. We either run the ball into the end zone or pass from the three-yard line for an extra two points—it's called a 2-point conversion.)

Jordan was stopped short for the 2-point conversion, but we were still ahead 6–0!

Churchill came right back and drove downfield for a score. Then they made their 2-point conversion. So we were behind 8–6 and in a real tough game.

The offense couldn't get in gear for the rest of the first half, even though I completed a couple of passes to Brandon. Coach gave Devro a few plays at quarterback, but he didn't do much. (I hope Coach didn't see me smiling under my helmet.)

Churchill scored another touchdown just before halftime, so we were behind 14–6 at halftime. Coach said I would start at quarterback in the second half.

We got off to a fast start in the second half when Devro took the kickoff and zigzagged his way to midfield. We charged downfield with Jordan banging into the line behind Colby and Brady. He scored on a two-yard dive.

We missed the 2-point conversion again, so we still trailed, 14–12.

The offense didn't make much progress until Devro made a nice punt return that gave us good field position with only a few minutes left. Devro is going to be great this season on kick returns. (Did you hear that, Coach? Kick returns, not quarterback!)

I stood on the sidelines half wondering if Coach Mack would play Devro or me at quarterback for the final few minutes. "Matt, get in there!" he shouted.

He didn't need to say it twice. I ran onto the field and into the huddle. "Come on," I told everybody as I buckled my chinstrap. "We need a touchdown on this drive."

We drove downfield, eating up yardage and time on the clock. I threw a couple of nice passes, but the rest were running plays. Jordan scored on a sweep around left end with Colby leading the way from 10 yards out.

We didn't get the extra points, but it didn't matter. We were ahead to stay, 18–14.

After the game I wanted to ask Michelle

if she could give me a copy of the game statistics. I figured I could put it in my journal. But I was worried she would think I just wanted to see my own stats.

I finally got up the courage to ask. I told her about the journal. Michelle thought it was a cool way to keep a record of the season. She sent the stats from her laptop to my phone. I'm telling you, Michelle knows everything about math...and computers.

GAME 1—CHURCHILL (9/23)

PASSING:	C/ATTS	YARDS	TDS	INTS
MONROE:	6/9	61	1	0
BEECH:	3/5	40	0	0
RUSHING:	**ATTS**	**YARDS**	**TDS**	
JENKINS:	17	75	2	
BEECH:	5	38	0	
RECEIVING:	**RECS**	**YARDS**	**TDS**	
GONZALEZ:	5	70	0	
CONSTANTINO:	3	18	1	

I completed six passes in nine attempts for 61 yards. One touchdown, no interceptions, and no fumbles. Not bad for a first game.

But look at Devro! He passed for 40 yards and ran for 38 more. That doesn't even count all the yards he gained returning kicks. The coaches are going to try to find ways to get him in the game. That's for sure.

And that's a problem...for me.

From: Ignacio.S@ParksideMS.WCPS.gov
Date: Sunday, September 26
To: MattQB7@Monroe37family.com

Matt—

Congratulations on your first win. I liked the way you put some dialog into your entries. You should do more of that.

I thought your descriptions of the game included a little too much play-by-play. But maybe that's because I'm not a football fan (thanks for explaining 2-point conversions). I would like to know more about the team than just what happens on the plays.

Remember, when you are describing anything—even a football game—to think of your five senses: sight, sound, smell, touch, and taste.

But you are right: your description of Elway's stomach problems went into too much detail.

Good luck against Western MS. Go, Parkside!

Ms. Samantha Ignacio
English Department
Parkside Middle School

As long as we have books, we are not alone.
—Laura Bush

Monday, September 27

Okay, when it comes to the five senses, smell is a big one in football. We've been practicing for three weeks and our huddle smells bad—like Elway when he really needs a bath.

I bet pro football players get their practice stuff cleaned every day. That doesn't happen at Parkside Middle School. The guys just stuff their dirty, smelly practice shirts and pants into their gym locker. The linemen are the worst—they don't care how they smell. After a while, even the inside of a player's helmet starts to reek because of the sweat.

Michelle was standing way over on the sidelines. "What's that smell?" she yelled.

"Is there a skunk loose somewhere?"

I mentioned to the guys during water break that maybe we should take our practice stuff home that night and wash it.

"No way!" Colby shouted. "We're undefeated. We can't wash our stuff. It might be bad luck."

"We've only played one game," I said.

"It doesn't matter," Colby insisted. "We got to keep everything exactly the same. At least until we lose."

"What if we never lose?" I asked.

Colby smiled and put his stinky, dirty arm around me. "Then our huddle is really going to reek. Just think of it as the smell of victory."

Tuesday, September 28

Coach Mack had us practice a trick play. I guess since we're playing Western this week and Bullis (they were undefeated last year) later in the season, he wants some way to score a quick touchdown.

Flare Right/Quarterback Pass Back is a pretty cool play. Here it is:

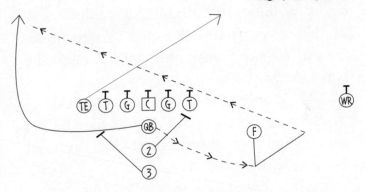

Flare Right
QB Pass Back

Devro lines up at quarterback while I line up on the right side as a flanker. When the ball is hiked, I take two or three quick steps straight back. Devro turns to the right and throws the ball *back* to me and then runs out for a pass. Because a ball that's thrown backward is not counted as a forward pass, I can chuck a pass to Devro or maybe Brandon.

The play might work. Hopefully, the defense won't notice that Devro and I have switched positions. Of course, we're not exactly twins, but our uniforms and helmets cover up a lot. But even if they do notice, the defense will probably think I'm going to run with the ball after Devro throws it to me.

We'll see. One problem: if the play works, the coaches might get the idea of keeping Devro at quarterback.

Friday, October 1

Some games come down to one play. Like the one we played yesterday. Both teams had trouble moving the ball during the first half. Every time I dropped back to pass, nobody was open, not even Brandon. And when I'd hand the ball off to Jordan...*wham!* He'd get tackled before he could get going.

The game was tied at halftime, 0–0.

In the second half, Western scored first after Jordan fumbled. We came back and scored on a nice run by Jordan after Devro had given us great field position with another long punt return. I hit Brandon with a pass for the 2-point conversion. We were ahead 8–6.

Western scored on a long pass. So now we were behind, 12–8, with not much time left. I knew this was our last chance to score.

Devro almost broke away on the kickoff return, but then he was tripped up at the 35-yard line. I hit Brandon with a couple of quick passes for a first down near midfield. We were moving the ball!

Jordan picked up another first down on a sweep to the left side. We were on Western's 38-yard line with less than two minutes to go.

Jordan got stopped cold, so it was second down and ten yards to go with the clock moving. I called Wide Right/Out and Up, my favorite pass play. That's when Brandon fakes a Down and Out and then takes off up the sideline.

"Give me enough time to get the pass off," I told the linemen. They did. Brandon faked the Down and Out and took off. He had a couple of steps on the Western corner-back so I was thinking touchdown when I let the ball go. But I threw the ball too high and it floated in the air too long. Brandon had to slow down and wait for the ball. That gave the Western cornerback time to catch up. They both leaped but the Western cornerback came down with the ball.

Interception! Western had the ball with less than a minute left. On the next play, their quarterback knelt down with the ball and let the clock run out. The game was over.

I was feeling so bad I decided not to ask Michelle for the game statistics. But she handed them to me just as I came off the field. "Tough game," she said.

GAME 2—WESTERN (9/30)

PASSING:	C/ATTS	YARDS	TDS	INTS
MONROE:	5/14	57	0	1
BEECH:	2/6	18	0	0
RUSHING:	**ATTS**	**YARDS**	**TDS**	
JENKINS:	20	55	1	
BEECH:	4	26	0	
RECEIVING:	**RECS**	**YARDS**	**TDS**	
GONZALEZ:	3	27	0	
CONSTANTINO:	2	12	0	

From: Ignacio.S@ParksideMS.WCPS.gov
Date: Sunday, October 3
To: MattQB7@Monroe37family.com

Matt—

Sorry to hear about the team's first loss. I enjoyed your description of the team's smelly huddle. It made me laugh. You also made good use of dialog.

Good luck on Thursday against Beverly.

Ms. Samantha Ignacio
English Department
Parkside Middle School

Ever tried? Ever failed? No matter. Try again. Fail again. Fail better.
—Samuel Beckett

Monday, October 4

Our offensive huddle did smell better today, but the defense wasn't happy. They kept bad-mouthing the offense, saying we only scored one touchdown. We told them they could talk when they shut down the other team!

I know it's because I'm the quarterback, but I think offensive players have a much tougher job. Learning all the plays and getting them right is hard. If just one person messes up, the play won't work. Every offensive player has to do his job exactly right. All the defense has to do is mess things up for the other team.

My grandfather always says that putting together a good offense is like building a house. Defense is like tearing a house down. "You can get anybody to tear a house down," he says. "But it's hard to find people who can build a house."

Wednesday, October 6

I think Coach Mack is getting nervous. He's working everybody extra hard this week. More calisthenics. More drills. More everything.

By the way, you know who loves calisthenics? Devro! The guy even likes leg lifts. He's always bouncing up and down, smiling really big, like he's going to Disney World or something. Brandon keeps telling me Devro just loves football. But I can't believe that. I mean *nobody* loves leg lifts.

I think Coach is stressed out because he knows we have to win this week against Beverly. Next week we play Bullis, and everybody thinks they are going to be the champs again this year. So if we want to have a chance at the championship, we better beat Beverly tomorrow.

And I better play well.

Thursday, October 7

It's late, but I couldn't wait until tomorrow to write about today's game. I like writing up the games...especially ones like this.

We killed Beverly 30–8! Best of all, I played great. I threw two touchdown passes to Brandon and a couple of 2-point conversions to Luke.

Beverly had nobody who could cover Brandon. He was open all day. They tried to double-team him, but it didn't matter. I hit him on Down and Outs, Slants, and Curl-Ins over the middle. It was like we were practicing at North Park in August in our shorts and T-shirts.

Greg and the rest of the line had a great game too. They gave me plenty of time to throw and they knocked the other team all over the place.

Michelle was smiling big time when she gave me the statistics after the game. I was smiling big time too.

GAME 3—BEVERLY (10/7)

PASSING:	C/ATTS	YARDS	TDS	INTS
MONROE:	12/16	181	2	0
BEECH:	2/3	28	0	0
RUSHING:	**ATTS**	**YARDS**	**TDS**	
JENKINS:	12	65	1	
BEECH:	6	32	0	
RECEIVING:	**RECS**	**YARDS**	**TDS**	
GONZALEZ:	9	136	2	
CONSTANTINO:	3	38	0	

Twelve completions in sixteen attempts. Two touchdowns and, most importantly, no interceptions. I played like Elway—the quarterback, not the dog!

I got to admit, Devro had a good game too. He completed a couple of passes and had some nice runs from scrimmage. But there was no doubt who was the MVP (Most Valuable Player) of this game. Me!

I love football.

And I love being the quarterback for Parkside Middle School.

From: Ignacio.S@ParksideMS.WCPS.gov
Date: Sunday, October 10
To: MattQB7@Monroe37family.com

Matt—

Congratulations on your big win and your excellent performance. But remember, the grade on your journal will not be based on your passing statistics, but on how well you describe what is happening to you and the team. Your entries this past week were shorter and had fewer details than the previous two weeks. Please remember to put more details into your writing.

Ms. Samantha Ignacio
English Department
Parkside Middle School

What is written without effort is in general read without pleasure.
—Samuel Johnson

Sunday, October 10

I am in BIG trouble. My playbook is gone. I've looked everywhere but I can't find it.

I haven't told my mom or dad because I know they would ask me the same stupid question people always ask: "Where's the last place you saw it?" If I could remember that, I would be able to find it.

I called Brandon to see if I had left it at his house. Nope.

"You're lucky tomorrow's a holiday," Brandon said, "We don't have school or football practice. We can spend the day looking for it."

I don't feel lucky. I feel dumb.

If Coach Mack finds out I lost my playbook, he'll be so mad at me. What if someone from another team, like Bullis, finds it? Coach might bench me and put Devro in at starting quarterback.

I have to find it!

Monday, October 11

I met Brandon around nine o'clock this morning. He wasn't in a good mood. He rubbed his eyes and yawned really big to make sure I knew he was tired.

"So, where was the last place you saw the playbook?"

"You sound like my mom," I snapped.

"Sometimes moms are right," Brandon said. He seemed impatient. "Think. Picture it in your hand. Where were you when you last had it?"

"I know I had it at school on Wednesday, after practice. Maybe I left it in the locker room."

"Let's start there," Brandon suggested.

He started walking, then stopped. "How will we get into the school?" he asked. "It's closed for Columbus Day, remember?"

"Mr. Samuels sometimes cleans on weekends and holidays, doesn't he?" I said. "He's cool. If he's there, maybe he'll let us in."

"We might as well give it a try," Brandon said as we headed toward the school. "I'll bet it's in the last place we look."

I don't know why, but that got me mad. "Why do people always say that?" I asked. "I mean, who would keep looking for something *after* they found it? Things are always in the last place you look."

"Hey, Mr. Genius, I'm not the guy who lost his playbook, remember?" Brandon said. "Let's get going."

In a few minutes we were standing in the bright sunshine at the entrance to Parkside Middle School. The front door was locked. When we peered through the windows, we didn't see Mr. Samuels, so we walked around to the back of the school. Brandon pulled at the door and it swung open. We looked at each other, kind of surprised. Then we laughed, but it was one of those nervous laughs.

"Come on," Brandon said. "Let's go."

I wanted to say, "Let's not," but I figured it was okay. We were just looking for my playbook. It wasn't like we were breaking in or trying to steal something.

It was strange being in the school when it was empty. The lights were dim and the corridors were almost dark. It was quieter than a study hall full of A students. The sounds of our sneakers squeaking against the floors echoed down the halls.

We were almost to the gym when we heard a shout.

"Hey, stop right there!"

We froze. My heart started pounding. I heard footsteps coming fast. I turned and saw someone running toward us. I felt better when I made out who it was.

"Hi, Mr. Samuels," Brandon said, trying to act cheery.

"What are you boys doing here?" Mr. Samuels asked. He didn't seem very happy to see us.

"We were looking for you," Brandon said quickly.

"On a holiday?" Mr. Samuels said. "Don't go playing games with me, young man. Tell me what you are doing here. Right now."

I was sweating like I'd done a million leg lifts. But I managed to explain how I'd lost my playbook and how I was hoping that I'd left it in the locker room.

Mr. Samuels lightened up a little after my explanation. "You boys would lose your heads if they weren't fastened to your necks," he said, rolling his eyes. "Come on, I'll take you down to the gym. Then you've got to get out of here."

Mr. Samuels unlocked the locker room with one of the keys he had on his belt. He walked over to Coach Mack's office and pulled out a large blue plastic bin. "Lost and found. Look in here."

Brandon and I reached into the bin. There were all kinds of shirts, socks, and school stuff. Brandon held up a pair of boxer shorts. "How can anybody forget their underwear?"

There were plenty of books in the bin. History books, comic books, a Harry Potter book, a science notebook, some sports magazines—everything but my playbook.

"Okay, it's not here," Mr. Samuels said, sounding impatient. "You guys got to get going. Now!"

We walked outside. The sunshine nearly blinded us after being in the dark hallway. We ran into Colby a few blocks from school. I explained my big problem to him.

"I saw Devro with a playbook after practice on Wednesday," Colby said. "Maybe he took it."

"Wait a second. How do you know it was Matt's playbook?" Brandon asked. "I mean Devro's got a playbook too."

"It had 'Quarterbacks Rule' on the cover, just like Matt's," Colby said. ""I bet you anything, Devro took it."

"I'll bet you're right. Let's find him," I said.

Colby nodded. "He usually plays hoops at North Park."

I was already walking. Sure enough,

when we got to the park, Devro was playing basketball with a bunch of seventh graders. I didn't waste any time and marched right onto the court. The game stopped. "Hey, Devro!" I shouted. "Where's my playbook?"

Devro turned toward me. "What are you talking about?" He sounded confused.

"You know what he's talking about," Colby said, stepping forward. "You took his playbook. I saw you."

Things got hot, real quick. We all started yelling stuff at each other—stuff that I can't put in my journal. For a second, I thought somebody was going to throw a punch.

"Everybody shut up!" Devro shouted above the noise. When we got quiet, he looked at me and said, "I gave your play-book to Michelle."

"Why'd you do that?" I yelled.

"I thought she'd give it to you," he said.

"How come she didn't?"

"I don't know. Ask her."

"Come on, Matt," Brandon whispered. "I think he's telling the truth."

Suddenly, I felt like a jerk. Part of me

wanted to tell Devro I was sorry. But I didn't want to look like a wimp in front of Brandon and Colby. Or a bunch of seventh graders. And, who knows, maybe Devro was lying.

"Let's get out of here," I said. Brandon, Colby, and I started to walk away. At the edge of the basketball court, I turned and shouted back, "Michelle better have my playbook!"

If she didn't, I wasn't sure what I would do.

Tuesday, October 12

Michelle walked up to me before school this morning and handed me my playbook. "Devro found it and gave it to me after practice last Wednesday," she said. "I would've given it to you sooner, but I put it in my backpack and forgot all about it."

"That's okay. I didn't miss it," I lied.

I saw Devro later at practice, but I didn't say anything for a bunch of reasons. First, because now I really felt like a jerk for accusing him of being a thief. Second, I didn't know what I would say. Third, if I didn't ask him about it again, he'd probably figure out that I got my playbook back.

Wednesday, October 13

It rained today. It was just a light drizzle when we started doing calisthenics. (I hate leg lifts on a regular day, but they are a hundred times worse lying on the ground with a wet butt.) The longer we played, the more it rained. By the end of practice it was coming down pretty hard.

I hate practicing in the rain. My uniform gets all wet and heavy. My feet get soaked too. The mud sticks to my cleats and oozes onto my socks.

The worst part is that the ball gets slick and slippery. It's hard to get any zip on my passes. It's even hard to get the hikes and handoffs right. The running backs and receivers were sliding all over the place. Brandon must have fallen ten times trying to run patterns. It was a mess.

But you know who loves the rain? The linemen. They were laughing and shouting the whole time. For guys like Colby and

Brady, it's like some big mud-wrestling match.

When practice ended they were covered and caked with mud. Colby took off his helmet, his white teeth shining on his muddy face. "That was an awesome practice," he declared.

I'll never understand linemen.

Saturday, October 16

I really don't want to write up the game this week. I wrote plenty already about losing my playbook. But it's part of the season, so I guess I should.

It's pretty simple: we stunk—worse than our huddle before the guys washed their practice stuff. Bullis pushed us all over the field. They were bigger, faster, and much better than we were.

Every time I handed the ball to Jordan, it was like he was running into a brick wall. *Bam!* When I faded back to pass, the Bullis defense was all over me. The only play that worked was Flare Right/Quarterback Pass Back—that trick play Coach put in a couple of weeks ago. It was second and long. (It seemed like it was second and long on every play.) I lined up at flanker and Devro called signals at quarterback. I don't think any of the Bullis players noticed we had switched positions. I guess they figured they could stop us no matter what we did.

Devro got the ball and I took three steps back, just like Coach Mack drew it up in the playbook. Devro passed the ball back to me and took off, sprinting past the defense.

When I looked up, it seemed like the whole Bullis team was charging at me. I couldn't see anything downfield. I just threw the ball where Devro was supposed to be. A split second later, the Bullis defense hammered me to the ground.

I never saw what happened. I was lying under about six Bullis guys. But I heard everybody on our sideline yelling and cheering. They kept it up long enough for me to realize that Devro must have gone all the way for a touchdown. As one of the Bullis players was getting up off me, he said, "That was a lucky play." I looked toward the end zone and there was Devro, bouncing around and slapping high fives with everybody.

The play was pretty lucky, but it didn't mean much. It just meant we lost 26–6 instead of 26–0.

Michelle almost forgot to give me the statistics and I almost forgot to ask. "Pretty ugly," she said as she finally handed them over.

GAME 4—BULLIS (10/14)

PASSING:	C/ATTS	YARDS	TDS	INTS
MONROE:	5/15	88	1	2
BEECH:	2/6	11	0	0
RUSHING:	**ATTS**	**YARDS**	**TDS**	
JENKINS:	12	25	0	
BEECH:	7	38	0	
RECEIVING:	**RECS**	**YARDS**	**TDS**	
GONZALEZ:	4	22	0	
BEECH:	1	60	1	

I'll say. Without that play to Devro, I would have been 4 out of 14 for 28 yards with two interceptions. Real ugly.

Devro's touchdown helped my statistics, though. After all, I threw the pass.

Sunday, October 17

Pop-Pop came over this weekend to watch the football games, and we got into a big discussion about who was the greatest quarterback of all time.

My grandfather said Johnny Unitas was the best. I didn't know much about Unitas, so I looked him up on Wikipedia. He *was* good. He won four MVP awards, played in ten Pro Bowls, and threw for more than 40,000 yards.

Pop-Pop is always talking about the old days in sports. Some kids get sick of adults talking about how great the players used to be, but I love to hear my grandfather talk about sports. He's been watching football forever. He even has a piece of a wooden goal post from a championship game he went to when he was a kid.

"What about Joe Montana or John Elway?" my dad asked. Every time he said

"Elway" our dog perked up his ears. I think he was hoping it was dinnertime.

My dad asked me to look up Montana and Elway on the Internet. I did. Here are their important career stats.

	ELWAY	MONTANA
Years	1983–1998	1979–1994
QB Rating	79.9	92.3
Yards	51,475	40,551
TDs	300	273
INTs	226	139
Super Bowls	5 (won 2)	4 (won 4)

They were good too. My dad always says he thinks Elway was the best. "He didn't have a great receiver like Jerry Rice to throw to, like Montana did."

I argued that Peyton Manning or Tom Brady were just as good as the quarterbacks who played when my dad and Pop-Pop were kids.

"Those guys were great," Pop-Pop admitted. "But not as great as Unitas," he quickly added.

We didn't settle the argument. But it was fun talking about it.

When Pop-Pop was leaving, he handed me the hardcover copy of a book called *Instant Replay*, by Jerry Kramer. It was so old the price on it was only $5.95!

"Your mom told me you were keeping a journal of your football season for English class," he said. "I thought you might like to see this. It was written by a guy who played in the 1960s for the Green Bay Packers. He kept a journal about his season just like you're doing."

"Really?" I could hardly believe someone got paid for writing a journal about football. "Did many people buy it?"

"Sure, it was a bestseller," Pop-Pop said. "How's your journal going?

"Good," I said. "I'm actually starting to like writing in it."

Pop-Pop nodded. He put on his winter coat and hat and started to go. At the front door he turned around and called back to me, "The Packers quarterback in that book—Bart Starr—he was pretty good too. But not as good as Unitas."

From: Ignacio.S@ParksideMS.WCPS.gov
Date: Sunday, October 17
To: MattQB7@Monroe37family.com

Matt—

Your journal entries are getting better all the time. I like the way you are adding more dialog now. Of course, I don't think you should have gone into the school on Columbus Day, but it was a terrific story. I am glad you found your playbook!

Keep up the good work. Remember to include more about your feelings in your journal.

By the way, I have heard of that book your grandfather gave you. My father read it years ago. He said he really enjoyed it.

Ms. Samantha Ignacio
English Department
Parkside Middle School

You can learn a line from a win and a book from a defeat.
—Coach Paul Brown

Monday, October 18

The coaches were super serious today at practice. They were saying things like, "We're starting all over again," and "Everybody is going to have to earn their playing time."

Coaches always talk like that. But we know we're not starting over. We have a 2–2 record. Two wins, two losses. There's nothing we can do about that. We have to win four games in a row to have a chance to play in the championship game. All the players know that. The coaches don't have to tell us.

Coach Mack worked us extra hard today. Lots of calisthenics. (I'll never ever get used to leg lifts!) Lots of drills. Especially block-ing and tackling drills.

Coach Shortall spent some time with me working on dropping back to pass. He says I have to do it faster. I think I got a little better at it.

I couldn't help noticing that the coaches gave Devro as many reps at quarterback as they gave me. Maybe they are thinking about making him the starter.

I know I'm supposed to write honestly about my feelings. Well, here's something honest about my feelings: I feel bad about accusing Devro of taking my playbook, but I feel terrible about Devro getting more reps at quarterback.

Tuesday, October 19

Devro usually sits with a couple of his seventh grade buddies in study hall, but today I saw that he was alone. I'd been thinking about apologizing for acting like a jerk, so I decided to talk to him before his buddies got there.

"How're you doing?" I asked as I sat

down, trying to act cool and casual.

"Okay," he said. He sounded like he didn't really want to talk to me.

"I want to say I'm sorry about the playbook mix-up." I could feel I was talking too fast, so I tried to slow down. "We just thought you might have taken it."

"Why would I do that?"

"You know, so you could get me in trouble and take over the quarterback spot."

"I don't have to take your playbook to do that."

That crack reminded me why I'm not a big Devro fan. He's so confident, so sure he's better than anybody. Including me. Brandon says I'm just jealous because Devro is such a good player. But why should I be jealous of Devro? I'm the starting quarterback.

"Forget it," I said as I got up to go to my seat. "I just wanted to say I'm sorry."

I'd better play well tomorrow. I'd hate losing my starting position to Devro. He'd never let me forget it.

Friday, October 22

Big game yesterday. We absolutely had to beat Falls Road to keep our chances alive to play in the championship game.

Thursday was warm, almost like summer was trying to hang on for one more day.

Coach Mack started me at quarterback. I was relieved because I knew he'd been thinking about playing Devro. I figured I'd better move the team as soon as we got the ball after the opening kickoff. On the first few plays I handed the ball to Jordan, who ran behind Colby's great blocking for a couple of first downs. We were moving.

I hit Brandon on a deep slant pass for a 15-yard gain. Two more runs and then I hit Luke with a perfect pass over the middle. He was tripped up just short of the goal line. On the next play Colby blasted a hole in their left side, and Jordan powered through it for a touchdown. Then he scored again for the 2-point conversion!

We were ahead 8–0.

Falls Road came right back. They had a fullback who looked like he had escaped from an NFL training camp. He was a complete beast! Falls Road drove downfield, pounding their big fullback into the middle of our defensive line. He broke through for a 20-yard touchdown run, dragging four of our guys across the goal line.

After the touchdown, the Falls Road fullback got up but didn't celebrate. Instead, he limped back to the sideline with a sprained ankle. The fullback didn't return. The guys on our defense didn't miss him one bit!

Falls Road didn't make the 2-point conversion and so we led 8–6.

Neither team did much on offense after the opening drives. Coach brought Devro in at quarterback, but Devro couldn't get us moving either. I can't say I felt bad about that.

Coach Mack seemed nervous during halftime. He yelled at us more than usual. "I thought *we* were ahead," Brandon whispered to me.

The Falls Road fullback was still on the sidelines at the beginning of the second half. Without their big star, the Falls Road offense fell apart. Our defense stopped them cold after the kickoff and they were forced to punt.

Jordan got us off to a fast start with a quick eight-yard gain. It was second down and two yards to go. Coach sent in Fake 36/ Wide Right Post. He was going for a big play.

I faked the ball to Jordan and faded back. Brandon was open over the middle. I reared back and fired. I was afraid I had overthrown him. But Brandon caught the ball on his fingertips and raced into the end zone.

Touchdown! We were ahead 14–6.

The score stayed that way until the fourth quarter. The Falls Road offense came alive and put together a long drive. Mixing up runs and short passes, our defense couldn't stop them. Even without their big fullback. When they crashed through for the touchdown, I could feel the momentum of the game changing.

They missed the 2-point conversion, but I still felt we were in trouble. "We better score on this drive," Brandon whispered to me on the sideline as Falls Road prepared to kick off.

Devro caught the kickoff at the 15-yard line, crashed into a wall of players at the 25-yard line, and spun loose. Suddenly free, he slipped by a tackler and started down the left sideline. As he sprinted past, Brandon and I jumped up and down on the sideline, screaming, "Go! Go! Go!"

Devro was going all...the...way!

Touchdown! We were ahead 20–12.

While everyone was celebrating on the sidelines, Coach Mack grabbed me by the pads. "Fake 35/Tight End Out," he ordered. "Do it right. Tell Jordan to really sell the fake."

The 2-point conversion was crucial. If we made it, we would be ahead by ten points and Falls Road would have to score twice to win.

I knelt down in the huddle. "Fake 35/ Tight End Out," I said, trying to stay calm. "Really sell the fake, Jordan. On two."

I faked a handoff to Jordan, who charged

into the line as if he had the ball. I pivoted to the right. I looked up, and there was Luke standing in the end zone, wide open. I tossed him the ball for an easy two points.

We were ahead to stay, 22–12.

Michelle was smiling when she handed me the stats. "With you passing, Brandon catching, Greg blocking, Jordan running, and Devro returning kicks," she said, "you guys are a pretty good team."

You know, I think she's right.

GAME 5—FALLS ROAD (10/21)

PASSING:	C/ATTS	YARDS	TDS	INTS
MONROE:	9/16	108	1	0
BEECH:	2/6	12	0	0
RUSHING:	**ATTS**	**YARDS**	**TDS**	
JENKINS:	14	62	1	
BEECH:	5	31	0	
RECEIVING:	**RECS**	**YARDS**	**TDS**	
GONZALEZ:	6	84	1	
CONSTANTINO:	3	21	0	

Saturday, October 23

Colby called tonight. "I've got a big problem," he said. "I think I might be flunking math."

That's more than a big problem. It's a disaster! If Colby flunks a course he can't play sports. Everyone knows that's the rule.

I can't believe it. Colby is a smart guy who gets good grades in his other subjects. He takes a real hard math class—advanced geometry. He's always complaining about his teacher, Mr. Veek. We call him "Veek the Geek" because all he ever talks about is math. (Sorry, Ms. Ig, but it's true.) I don't think he even knows Parkside has a football team. There's no way Mr. Veek is going to cut Colby a break just because he plays football.

If we lose Colby, our season is over. He's our best offensive lineman, by far. We gain lots of yards running Jordan to the left side behind Brady and Colby, especially Colby. I don't even want to think about playing the championship game against Bullis without him.

The way we're playing, we definitely

70

have a chance to play in the championship game. But only *if* we still have Colby.

Sunday, October 24

I was lying in bed this morning trying to think of a way to help Colby pass advanced geometry when it hit me.

Michelle!

She's super smart at math. She has an A-plus average in the same class. She's the team manager, and the manager is supposed to help the team. Making sure Colby passes would be a huge help.

So I called her. I felt kind of weird asking her if she would help Colby. But she was real nice about it and even suggested they start tomorrow—they have a study hall together. Michelle said they would have to work fast because two big tests were coming up in the next two weeks.

Then I called Colby. At first he didn't like the idea. "You told Michelle I'm flunking?" he asked. "Thanks for making me look like an idiot." It's weird. Colby didn't say anything about messing up in front of his mom and dad and Mr. Veek. He didn't seem all that worried about letting down all his teammates and the coaches. The one thing that made him feel really bad was that Michelle might think he was dumb.

But I managed to talk him into it. Now it's all set. Michelle is going to help Colby with his math.

I just hope it works.

From: Ignacio.S@ParksideMS.WCPS.gov
Date: Sunday, October 24
To: MattQB7@Monroe37family.com

Matt—

Your entries last week were well written, with lots of colorful details. I hope you don't lose Colby. Now I know how important a good offensive line is.

By the way, Mr. Veek is very nice. Most students don't know this, but he is on a competitive Ultimate Frisbee team. But you're right; he's not a football fan.

Ms. Samantha Ignacio
English Department
Parkside Middle School

Outside of a dog, a book is man's best friend. Inside a dog, it's too dark to read.
—Groucho Marx

Monday, October 25

When my lunch period was over, I went by study hall to see if Colby was working with Michelle. Sure enough, they were sitting in a quiet corner away from everybody. They had their heads buried in a math book. Colby didn't look like he was complaining about "Veek the Geek" to Michelle. He looked like he was paying attention and trying his hardest.

He was really dressed up...at least for Colby. Instead of his usual baggy sweats and faded Packers T-shirt, He was wearing jeans and a new-looking shirt. Even his hair was different. I didn't know Colby owned a comb.

We had practice today. Same old stuff.

Tuesday, October 26

I guess Coach Mack figured we were tired of practice because he changed things today—big time.

"No pads," he said as he stuck his head into the locker room. "Just come out in your sweats."

When we got to the field, Coach Mack and Coach Shortall had divided it into four smaller playing fields with lines of plastic orange cones. They split us into eight teams with six kids on a team. They really mixed things up. They put offensive and defensive players on teams together as well as seventh and eighth graders.

"No practice today. Instead, we're going to have a touch football tournament," Coach Mack announced, holding a football above his head. Everybody cheered.

"One-hand touch, no more than three receivers can go out on a play," Coach explained. "And just to make things interesting, the teams have to change the quarterback on every play. Everybody gets a turn at that position."

The games were an absolute blast. We spent a sunny afternoon running around, yelling and screaming, making up plays, throwing passes, and tossing crazy laterals. It reminded me of why I love playing football. We played until it got dark. Nobody wanted practice to end.

Devro's team won the tournament. I hate to admit it, but he can do anything on a football field. It doesn't matter what position he plays, he's great at it. That kid can pass, run, catch passes, and play defense. And whatever Devro's doing, he seems happy doing it. Maybe Brandon's right about him. Maybe Devro is just crazy about football.

My team lost every game. But that didn't matter. I discovered that defensive players aren't very good at throwing or catching passes. Of course, they discovered that I'm lousy at playing defense. I guess we need all kinds of players to be a good team.

Maybe that was Coach Mack's plan all along.

Wednesday, October 27

A funny thing happened in study hall today. Brandon and I got into a big argument with a couple of guys on the Parkside soccer team about which sport is tougher to play, football or soccer.

Sam Donohue and Martin Mendoza were bragging that soccer players have to be in great shape. "Soccer is nonstop action," Sam said. "No time to rest. We don't have a huddle after every play like in football."

I could tell Brandon was getting mad. "So what?" he said. "You don't have somebody beating you up every play."

"What are you talking about?" Martin said. "Soccer is rough. Look at this." He pulled up his pants leg to show us all his bruises.

Brandon wasn't impressed. "My whole body looks like that," he said.

"Same with me." I said. "Anyway, not every guy in soccer is running the whole game. When the ball's near the other team's goal, the defensive players stand around taking it easy."

"Yeah? What about football linemen?" Sam asked.

"What about them?"

"They're fat. You never see a fat soccer player."

"You want to tell Colby Johnson he's fat?" I dared him.

That shut them up, but only for a minute. Sam came back with, "The World Cup is the most popular sporting event in the world."

"So what?" Brandon blurted out. "Most countries only play soccer."

I guess we were getting too loud because Ms. Leeds (my English teacher last year) came over to our table and told us to keep it down. I asked Ms. Leeds which sport she thought was better, soccer or football.

She thought for a minute and said, "Baseball."

"Baseball? Why baseball?"

"Because more good books have been written about baseball."

Just like a teacher! They never stop trying to teach you something, even when you're not their student anymore.

No touch football today at practice. Coach Mack was all business getting us ready for tomorrow's game against Robert Frost. The school, not the poet.

We could beat the poet. He's dead.

Thursday, October 28

Everything started great against Robert Frost. But things changed quickly—in a way I never expected.

We got the opening kickoff and moved down the field. I hit Brandon with a couple of quick passes and Jordan had some nice runs. It was first and ten on the 22-yard line. I took a chance and called my favorite pass play, Wide Right/Out and Up. Brandon faked out the cornerback, and I hit him for an easy touchdown. I tossed a quick slant to Brandon for the 2-point conversion and we were ahead, 8–0.

We scored again late in the first half when Brandon ran a deep post pattern and got past the Robert Frost safety. I fired him a perfect pass right over the middle and he raced in for the TD.

So we were ahead 14–0 at halftime. Even Coach Mack seemed calm. He barely yelled at us.

But in the second half, one play changed everything.

We had the ball near midfield. We were driving again. It was second down, eight yards to go. I figured I'd try another pass to Brandon. I called Wide Right/Square-In. Brandon ran straight for ten yards and cut sharply toward the middle of the field. I saw him out of the corner of my eye and threw.

The ball slapped into Brandon's hands and he pulled it tight against his chest. Before he could take another step, three Robert Frost defenders hit him high and low at the same time.

Some of the guys said later they heard something go *pop!* I didn't hear that sound, but I did hear Brandon screaming. When I got a clear view of him, he was lying on his back in the dirt, twisting back and forth.

His left hand was reaching down to his left leg. His right hand was still wrapped around the football.

I pushed my way through the circle of players gathered around him.

Dr. Tran ran out onto the field. She got Brandon to stop squirming and to hold still. After a few seconds, he stopped screaming. He pounded the ground with his left fist. The ball was cradled in his right arm. He didn't want to let go of it.

The eye black on his cheeks was wet and smeared. It might have been from the sweat, but I think he was crying. I've known Brandon my whole life and I'd never seen him cry. Ever. Not even when his dog died.

Dr. Tran told everybody to step back. When she turned to speak to Coach Mack, I thought I heard the words "broken ankle" and "hospital."

I don't remember much of the game after that. We had to keep playing even though we didn't want to. The offense struggled without Brandon. We made a few first downs with Jordan running. Devro came in for a while and completed some short passes. But we didn't come close to another touchdown. Luckily, our defense played great and only let up one touchdown with less than a minute to go.

When Michelle brought over the stat sheet, I barely looked at it.

GAME 6—ROBERT FROST (10/28)

PASSING:	C/ATTS	YARDS	TDS	INTS
MONROE:	11/18	122	2	1
BEECH:	3/3	40	0	0
RUSHING:	**ATTS**	**YARDS**	**TDS**	
JENKINS:	20	77	0	
BEECH:	4	33	0	
RECEIVING:	**RECS**	**YARDS**	**TDS**	
GONZALEZ:	6	98	2	
CONSTANTINO:	4	38	0	

"I wonder how Brandon's doing," she said.

I shook my head, remembering Brandon's screams. "It didn't look good. He's probably out for the season."

We won 14–8. We still have a chance to

play in the championship game. Our record is 4–2. But it's funny, when your best friend gets hurt, it feels like you're 0–6.

Friday, October 29

I was as nervous today about Colby's test as I am before a big game. I saw Colby and Michelle in the hall after their math class. "How was the test?" I asked.

Colby tried to act all cool and confident, especially in front of Michelle. "Not bad," he said.

Michelle shrugged after Colby walked down the hall with a bunch of the football linemen. "It was a pretty tough test," she said. "It's going to be close."

I got nervous all over again. I looked at Michelle.

"I guess we'll find out next week," she said.

Sunday, October 31 (Halloween)

This doesn't have anything to do with football, but I thought it would be fun to write about something else for a change.

I know I'm getting kind of old for it, but I still like going out on Halloween. I don't get all dressed up in a costume, I just put on some old clothes and a beat-up hat. Then I rub some dirt on my face and go as a bum.

My mom has never been all that big into Halloween. When I was little, I wore the same outfit for five years straight. My mom took an old brown skirt and sewed elastic at the top and bottom. She attached something that looked like laces along the front and cut out a place for each of my arms. Then she put the costume on me so my head poked out and said, "You're a football." I asked, "But shouldn't I be puffier? Footballs are round." She said, "You're a *deflated* football."

As I got bigger, the football covered less and less of me. I pointed this out to my mom, thinking she would make me another costume. She just told me, "You're a mini football." I was cool with that. I just wanted the candy.

The big reason to go out on Halloween in my neighborhood is Ms. Roberts's house.

Her kids are grown, but she still loves fixing her place up for Halloween.

Her house is set way back from the street, and her front yard has lots of overgrown bushes and big trees with drooping branches. Ms. Roberts hangs fake spiders, skeletons, and other creepy stuff from the trees. She plays a recording of strange noises and people screaming.

The year I turned eight, I ran ahead of the other kids and got to her place first. The trees were decked out with the usual creepy stuff, the way they were every Halloween, but the house was quiet and only the porch light was on. It looked like Ms. Roberts wasn't home.

She had placed a big bowl of candy on the lap of a scarecrow that was propped up in a chair in the front yard, close to the porch stairs. A handwritten sign hanging around the scarecrow's neck said:

Sorry, not home.
Help yourself to one piece of candy.

I headed up the dark walk in my football costume and saw the scarecrow and the sign. I reached into the bowl to take a Snickers bar.

Suddenly, the scarecrow jumped to life. It grabbed me with its straw-stuffed arms and screamed, "Now I've got you!"

It was Ms. Roberts! She had put on a mask and dressed up as a scarecrow to trick the kids in the neighborhood. It sure worked with me. I was so scared I thought I would pee in my football costume.

Ms. Roberts was real nice afterwards. She gave me an extra Snickers bar. She asked me not to tell the other neighborhood kids so she could surprise them too. I promised I wouldn't tell them. I was smiling when I left her house that night, but I never went back there by myself.

Brandon couldn't go out with us tonight because of his broken ankle, so Colby and I dressed up like bums and went over to Ms. Roberts's house to check it out. There weren't any scarecrows or skeletons in her yard or strange sounds coming from her house. The lights were on, though, so we went to the door.

We rang her bell and shouted "Trick or Treat!" Ms. Roberts came to the door wearing a black witch hat but nothing really scary.

"You're not doing anything for Halloween this year?" I asked her.

Ms. Roberts smiled. "Sorry guys, not this year, I've been too busy at work."

Greg and I took our candy and thanked her. We walked back down the front walk, ducking under the low-hanging tree branches, feeling kind of disappointed.

Just as we got halfway to the street, a huge, hairy monster dropped out of a tree and almost hit me on the head. A wild, crazy laugh—*Bwa-ha-ha-ha-ha!*—came from Ms. Roberts's house.

The Queen of Halloween had tricked me again. I was so scared I almost peed in my bum's clothes.

(I guess it's like you said, Ms. Ig: You've got to keep your eyes open. Things aren't always what they seem.)

From: Ignacio.S@ParksideMS.WCPS.gov
Date: Sunday, October 31
To: MattQB7@Monroe37family.com

Matt—

Nice job with the Halloween story. I'm glad to see you branching out.

I was so sorry to hear about Brandon. I hope he gets better quickly. But I will be interested to hear how his injury affects the team. Who will play wide receiver?

I may attend the game at Renwich Middle. I live nearby. I will be very interested in your impressions of the school.

Don't forget that next Friday will be the last opportunity for writing in your journal.

Ms. Samantha Ignacio
English Department
Parkside Middle School

*You cannot open a book without learning
something.*
—Confucius

Tuesday, November 2

Coach Mack put the league standings on the locker room bulletin board today. We're 4 and 2, tied for second place. Bullis, of course, is undefeated and in first place.

Coach said if we win our next two games against Renwich and Lampeter, we'll have a chance to play Bullis in the championship game. They're the same guys who pounded us 26–6. Some reward.

In the middle of practice, I saw Devro talking to Coach Mack on the sidelines. Colby noticed it too. "Better watch out," he said. "I'll bet Devro's telling Coach that he should be playing QB instead of you since Brandon's hurt."

Yeah, I bet Devro's thinking that now that our best receiver is done for the season, the coaches may want a quarterback like him who can run, instead of a quarterback like me who can throw.

So I kept one eye on Devro during practice. I was thinking about him so much, I had a lousy practice. I must have missed a million passes.

Coach Mack and Coach Shortall spoke to Devro a couple more times between drills. Nothing that unusual, but I decided to talk to him when practice ended.

"Okay, that's it. Good practice today!" Coach Mack shouted as it got dark. "See you tomorrow. Be ready to work."

The team walked slowly across the field to the school. I caught up to Devro. "I saw you talking to Coach Mack," I said and I didn't sound too friendly. "Are you still trying to take my job as starting quarterback?"

Devro stopped in his tracks. "Will you give me a break, man?" he said, shaking his head. "I was asking Coach Mack if I could take Brandon's spot at wide receiver. I thought I could help the team by catching a few touch-downs." He broke into a jog, leaving me standing there feeling like a jerk again.

Reading back over this journal entry, I can see why. I was acting like a jerk.

Maybe Brandon's been right all along. Maybe Devro doesn't want to play quarter-back—he just wants to *play*.

Wednesday, November 3

Colby took his last math test today. We'll find out next week whether he'll be eligible to play the last game of the season and the championship game—if we make it that far.

I saw Michelle in the hall after lunch. "How was the test?" I asked.

"Easier than the last one," she said. "He should be okay."

I hope she's right. I wouldn't want to play Bullis without Brandon *and* Colby! If we do, I'll end up like Brandon. Except my cast won't be on my ankle, it will be over my whole body.

The big news is that Coach Mack is play-ing Devro at Brandon's old position. I guess

Devro really was asking Coach if he could play wide receiver.

After practice, Devro came to me and suggested we stick around to work on pass patterns. He wasn't all buddy-buddy about it, just talking straight. Still, I felt funny hanging out with him. After all, he is taking the place of my best friend on the team.

But he's right. It will help the team if he plays wide receiver. He's super fast and catches anything near him.

It took a while to get my timing down with Devro. He's faster than Brandon, so I had to throw the ball more out in front of him.

We stayed an extra half hour working on pass patterns. Down and Outs, Slants, Out and Ups, just the way Brandon and I did over the summer at North Park. Devro and I didn't talk much. Coach Shortall stood on the sidelines watching us.

The air was cold. I kept blowing on my hands but my fingertips were getting numb. It was getting dark. The only light came from the school and the streetlights around the parking lot. When Devro went long, I could barely see him.

Finally, we called it quits and headed for the locker room. As we walked toward the school I looked around the practice field. The dark, the cold, the hard ground—it all made me realize that winter was coming and the season was slipping away.

"Good hands," I said and put out my fist. Devro tapped it with his. I thought I saw him smile.

Maybe I've been wrong about this guy.

Thursday, November 4

Renwich Middle School is about 25 miles from Parkside in a town where the houses are all big and set far apart from one another. The campus is huge and the athletic fields are awesome. The guys on our team call the place "Real Rich Middle School."

The high school is also on this campus. I guess that's why everything is so perfect. The baseball stadium looks like something out of the major leagues.

The bowl-shaped football stadium is cool too. It must seat 5000 people. The grass on the field is perfect, as if nobody has ever played on it.

The stands were packed with Renwich parents and students. They all wore their school colors and had a ton of school spirit. I've never seen so many people wearing green and gold. They all stood and cheered when the Renwich team came running onto the field. After everyone stood and sang "The Star-Spangled Banner," they boomed out their school song—something about always being true to Renwich.

"Does Parkside even have a school song?" Colby whispered to me on the sidelines.

If we do, I've never heard it.

Then the game started. And you know what? Those guys from Renwich couldn't play a lick.

Their team kicked off. Devro took the ball at about the 10-yard line, faked left, cut through the middle, and sprinted untouched to the end zone.

Touchdown!

I looked up at the big, beautiful Renwich scoreboard and clock (donated by the class of 2008). It had taken 15 seconds for us to take the lead. We got the 2-point conversion on Jordan's run straight up the gut.

The game had barely started and we were ahead, 8–0.

Our defense stopped Renwich cold and they had to punt. We took over on the 32-yard line and drove downfield mostly on running plays. Finally, on first down I faked the ball to Jordan, faded back, and saw Devro wide open, ten yards in back of the nearest Renwich defender. It was like playing catch. Devro could have walked into the end zone.

The score was now 16–0.

We would have won 60–0 if Coach Mack had wanted to run up the score. But he used the game to play lots of second-string kids. We still won 38–0.

I have to hand it to the "Real Rich" kids, though. They played hard the whole game. The fans kept cheering and stayed in the stands even when it began to rain. (They all pulled out green and gold umbrellas). When the game was over, they stood up again and sang that song about being true to Renwich.

It was kind of weird, but kind of cool.

Maybe Parkside should get a school song. Or team umbrellas.

GAME 7—RENWICH (11/4)

PASSING:	C/ATTS	YARDS	TDS	INTS
MONROE:	13/16	161	3	1
PARKER:	3/6	32	1	0
RUSHING:	**ATTS**	**YARDS**	**TDS**	
JENKINS:	7	65	0	
EDWARDS:	12	56	1	
RECEIVING:	**RECS**	**YARDS**	**TDS**	
BEECH:	6	105	2	
CONSTANTINO:	5	58	1	

From: Ignacio.S@ParksideMS.WCPS.gov
Date: Sunday, November 7
To: MattQB7@Monroe37family.com

Matt—

   I enjoyed the Renwich game. You played very well. I also enjoyed reading your journal entry about the school. The details you used to describe the campus were excellent.

   Your journal has greatly improved since the beginning of the year. Good work. I knew you could do it.

Ms. Samantha Ignacio
English Department
Parkside Middle School

You don't write because you want to say something; you write because you have something to say.
—F. Scott Fitzgerald

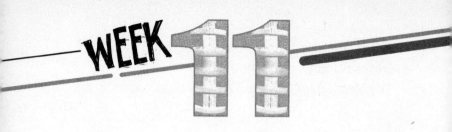

Monday, November 8

My assignment for Ms. Ig is finished. I don't have to keep a journal anymore—for her anyway. But I want to keep writing for me—at least until the end of the season. That way I'll have a complete record of it.

Tuesday, November 9

The school posted report cards on the school website today. I did fine. I even got an A in English. I guess Ms. Ig wasn't lying when she said she liked my journal.

I saw Colby and Michelle in the hall after first period. They were both smiling. "I passed advanced geometry," Colby said. "I can play!"

"He got a 92 on the last test," Michelle added proudly.

"A 92?" I couldn't believe it.

"Yeah," Colby said. "I almost beat Michelle."

"Not quite," Michelle said. "I got 102 on my test."

"How can you get more than 100%?" I asked.

"Extra credit."

That girl is super good at math.

Practice was fun today because everyone was still feeling psyched about our big win against Renwich. Devro and I stayed late again, practicing pass patterns.

That guy's as good at football as Michelle is at math. He's fast. He can catch the ball. He can throw the ball.

I don't think we'll ever be best friends, but he is awesome to play with—as long as I'm the quarterback!

Wednesday, November 10

I went over and sat down with Devro in study hall today. He didn't seem thrilled about it until I explained why I was there.

"I've been thinking," I said. "We've been practicing patterns after practice for a while now, and I know you're a good passer, especially on the run. So I think we should have a play where you throw a pass."

"You want *me* to play quarterback?" Devro asked in disbelief.

"Not exactly." I got out a piece of paper and sketched out a trick play.

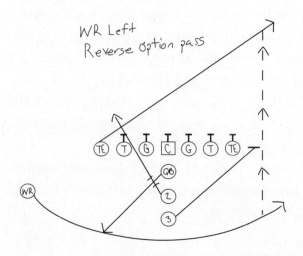

"We could call it something like Wide Receiver Left/Reverse/Option Pass," I said.

"You line up on the left as a wide receiver and come around and get a handoff from me as if you're running a reverse. Except instead of running, you'll throw a pass. Luke will run a long slant pattern from tight end toward the right sideline."

Devro studied the play for a few seconds and then grabbed the pen from my hand. "You could even run out to the left side after you hand the ball off to me," he said.

"It might work," I said. "You're good at throwing the ball on the run and Luke is fast enough to slip behind the defensive backs. Maybe we can catch the Bullis defense by surprise."

"Okay," Devro said. "Let's show the play to Coach Mack at practice next week."

"But first we've got to beat Lampeter tomorrow," I said.

"No sweat. We'll beat 'em."

Just like Devro—always super confident. But now I don't mind so much. I figure his being confident is good for the team— and for me.

Thursday, November 11

I felt bad during the Lampeter game today. I kept looking at Brandon standing on the sidelines in his heavy winter coat with his crutches. I know he wants to play. And I wish he could.

But Devro is a *great* wide receiver.

He showed it on the first drive. I noticed the Lampeter cornerback was playing about eight yards off Devro. I guess that's what Ms. Ig means when she says, "Keep your eyes open." So I called Flare Pass/Right. I got the ball and fired a quick pass to Devro on the right flat. Devro caught the ball and did the rest. He faked out the cornerback, dashed down the sideline, and then cut back to avoid some tacklers and outraced everyone to the end zone.

He's amazing. He ran 60 yards from the line of scrimmage!

His other two touchdowns were on similar plays. One was on a quick, five-yard Square-In pattern, where Devro spun away from a couple of Lampeter defensive backs and was gone.

The third touchdown was really cool. I noticed the Lampeter cornerback was creeping up on Devro, playing him a step or two closer. So I made up a play in the huddle. I called it Fake Flare Right and Go. "Run it just like Flare Pass/Right," I told Devro. "I'll fake it to you and then take off."

The play worked great. I pivoted as if I were going to throw the ball to Devro on the flat again. He turned and stood there with his hands open as if he were ready to catch the ball. The Lampeter defensive back came racing up, and Devro took off down the sideline. I hit him in stride about ten yards beyond the line of scrimmage. And as Brandon had learned during the mile run at the beginning of the season, *nobody* catches Devro.

Touchdown!

We needed every one of Devro's touchdowns. Lampeter was good. They kept the game close and moved the ball against our defense.

But we had Devro. His last TD put us ahead to stay and we won 30–24.

When Michelle brought over the statistics after the game, I barely looked at mine. I was too amazed by Devro's stats to notice anything else.

GAME 8—LAMPETER (11/11)

PASSING:	C/ATTS	YARDS	TDS	INTS
MONROE:	13/20	233	3	1
RUSHING:	**ATTS**	**YARDS**	**TDS**	
JENKINS:	16	51	0	
EDWARDS:	5	19	1	
RECEIVING:	**RECS**	**YARDS**	**TDS**	
BEECH:	9	207	3	
CONSTANTINO:	3	18	0	

"Wow," I said. "Nine receptions. Three touchdowns. And look. More than 200 yards receiving."

"He also brought back the kickoffs and punts for at least another 100 yards," Michelle reminded me.

"He was the whole team," I said.

"You did pretty well," Michelle said. "You threw for more than 200 yards."

"I hardly did anything except keep my

eyes open—and watch Devro."

I looked at the stats again and shook my head. After this, Brandon may never get his wide receiver job back.

Friday, November 12

I went to the Whitman High School football game tonight with Brandon. We met Colby and found a place in the corner of the stands where it wasn't so crowded. Brandon sat on the aisle where he could straighten out his leg that was still in a cast.

The game was awesome. While the school band played, the Whitman team came running out between two lines of cheerleaders and crashed right through a big homemade banner.

"Man, they're big," Colby said as he eyed the players.

"Yeah, you better start working out," I warned him.

"What do you mean *I* better start working out? *You* better start working out. They're gonna be tackling *you*."

The captains from both teams met in

the middle of the field for the coin toss. I noticed one of the Whitman captains was on crutches. "Hey look, Brandon. That's you in a couple years."

"Shut up. The doctor says I should be good as new in a couple *months*."

Actually, I was thinking it would be totally cool to be one of the Whitman football captains in three years. I'd be throwing passes to Brandon—and Devro. He's a year behind us, so he'd be a junior then. They would make a great pair of wide receivers.

The stands at Whitman are on one side of the field. The rest of the field is surrounded by tall, dark-green trees. As the game went on, the sky grew darker and the trees turned almost black. The field and players seemed to glow beneath the Friday night lights.

Lots of people turned out to watch the game. The stands were full with most of the parents and kids crowding into the seats closest to the 50-yard line. And more fans were standing in back of the end zone where the booster club was selling hot dogs, candy, and drinks.

After the game began, I concentrated on the quarterbacks. I watched the way they dropped back to pass and how they handed the ball off, called the plays, and ran the offense. I noticed a million things I'm going to have to improve if I want to play quarterback in high school.

Brandon watched the wide receivers and Colby studied the line play. The game was much faster and rougher than our freshman team games. Even in the stands we could hear pads and helmets crashing together.

At halftime, I went to the snack bar with Colby to get some hot chocolate. Brandon stayed behind because of his leg.

I saw Devro and some of his seventh-grade buddies laughing as they waited in line. "You still feeling good about your three touchdowns?" I called out.

Devro smiled. "Yeah. And I'm hoping you'll throw me some more."

"Don't worry," I said. "I will."

After I paid for the hot chocolate, I stood near the end zone and took in the whole scene. The lights. The dark sky and darker trees. The band marching off the field. The smell of hot dogs sizzling on the grill. Kids walking around, talking on their phones. Cheerleaders shouting into the night. Parents huddled in the stands under their winter blankets. The *click-click* of the players' cleats against the pavement as they jogged back onto the field for the second half.

The cups of hot chocolate felt warm in my hands.

I can't wait to play under the lights for Whitman High School with Brandon and Colby—and Devro.

From: Mack.R@ParksideMS.WCPS.gov
Date: Sunday, November 14
To: MattQB7@Monroe37family.com

Dear Parkside football player:

As you know, we finished with a record of 6–2 this season and tied for second place with Western Middle School. Consistent with the league rules, the Parkside and Western coaches met and flipped a coin to determine who would meet Bullis in the championship game on Thursday, November 18.

Parkside won the coin toss, and so we will play in the championship game. Please report to practice at 3 p.m. tomorrow. Be ready to work hard.

Go, Parkside!

Coach Robert Mack
Athletic Department
Parkside Middle School

It's not whether you get knocked down, it's whether you get up.
—Coach Vince Lombardi

Monday, November 15

Coach Mack had us practice our old trick play today—the one where Devro is at quarterback and I'm at wide receiver.

We also practiced my (and Devro's) trick play—Wide Receiver Left/Reverse/Option Pass. Coach Mack wasn't real thrilled about the play at first. But lucky for us, Coach Shortall spoke up. "Why don't we try it?" he said. "We're going to need something new against Bullis."

The play worked pretty well. Devro is so good at throwing on the run that he put the ball in Luke's hands every time. He even threw one back to me running down the left sideline. Who knows? Coach might even use the play in the Bullis game.

Tuesday, November 16

I stayed up late the last two nights finishing *Instant Replay*, that football book about the 1967 Green Bay Packers. It's written by Jerry Kramer, who was an All-Pro offensive guard for the Packers.

One thing I noticed: Kramer didn't write the book. Instead, he talked into a tape recorder a couple of times a week and then sent the tapes to Dick Schaap, a sportswriter. Schaap wrote up the notes and sat down with Kramer after the season so Kramer could add some more thoughts. I should have asked Ms. Ig if I could have talked into a tape recorder and sent my stuff to a sportswriter. Of course, it's fun *being* the sportswriter too.

Once I got started reading, I couldn't stop. Kramer talks a lot about the team, their practices, and their games. But he also told some interesting stories about their coach, Vince Lombardi. Coach Mack can be pretty tough, but this guy Lombardi was murder. He worked the 1967 team really hard. The previous year the Packers had won the first Super Bowl ever played, and Lombardi was determined for the Packers to win Super Bowl II. But first the team had to face the Dallas Cowboys in the NFL championship game.

That game was unbelievable. It was played in Green Bay, Wisconsin. The temperature was 13 degrees *below* zero. The wind made it feel like 30 or 40 degrees below! Most of the players wore gloves and long underwear to try to stay warm. The heaters on the sidelines that were supposed to keep the players warm broke down. The field was as hard as rock.

The Cowboys were ahead, 17–14. The Packers got the ball with five minutes left. They drove the ball to the one-yard line with sixteen seconds left. (Pop-Pop was right: the Packers quarterback, Bart Starr, was really good.) The Packers decided to go for the touchdown instead of kicking a field goal to tie the game. The championship came down to one play.

Kramer had noticed from studying game film that the Cowboys defensive tackle,

Jethro Pugh, had trouble getting down low in his stance because he was so tall. I guess Kramer was keeping his eyes open, too, just like Ms. Ig told me to do. Kramer figured he could come out low and move Pugh back just enough—especially on the icy field—for Bart Starr to slip into the end zone on a Quarterback Sneak.

And that's what the Packers did. Kramer blasted Pugh back and Starr snuck the ball into the end zone. The Packers won 21–17.

The Packers went on to win Super Bowl II against the Oakland Raiders, 33–14, but the game everyone remembered was the one against the Cowboys. They called it "The Ice Bowl." Kramer became the most famous lineman around because the television networks showed the play where he threw the game-winning block against Pugh over and over again on instant replay.

I was thinking how cool it would be if our season ended like that. Maybe we'll beat Bullis on the last play of the game. And, just like Jerry Kramer, I'll be the hero!

Wednesday, November 17

During one of our drills I realized that whether we win or lose tomorrow, today was the last day of football practice.

After we went through all the plays we might use in the game—including Wide Receiver Left/Reverse/Option Pass—Coach Mack called everyone together. We knelt in a big circle with our helmets off. My ears were burning from the cold. Coach gave us a long pep talk about how we can beat Bullis if we just believe in ourselves. He even quoted that Vince Lombardi guy a couple of times.

After a while I zoned out and looked around the huddle. Colby, Brady, Jordan, Luke, Devro—all the guys. Brandon stood at the edge of the circle on his crutches next to Michelle. I wished he could play.

I thought about all the stuff that had happened during the season. The wins. The losses. The touchdown passes. The trick plays. And that last-minute interception I threw against Western. (Man, I still wish I had that play back.)

I thought about the day I couldn't find my playbook. The times I worried that the coaches might play Devro instead of me at quarterback. Colby almost flunking math and Michelle saving the day. Brandon's injury and the way he was rolling on the ground screaming. I thought about how wrong I was about Devro. It turned out he wasn't such a bad guy after all. He really stepped in and did a great job at wide receiver.

The whole season seemed to go by so fast. I'm glad I kept the journal so I'll be able to remember it all.

When I tuned back in, Coach Shortall was saying something about how we could beat Bullis. I don't know, maybe we can. It'll be tough. To be honest, we'll have to get lucky. They're better than we are. But sometimes you have to play teams that are better.

When the coaches finished talking, we all got up and walked to the locker room. The night was cold and dark. It's winter now, for real. I could feel the cold right through my football gear. I was thinking how good a hot shower was going to feel.

But somehow I couldn't make myself hurry off the field. I walked slowly, very slowly, toward the locker room door.

I'm going to miss football.

Thursday, November 18

Today was a perfect day to play football. The sun was shining. The temperature was around 50 degrees. There was almost no wind.

We grabbed the lead early. On our first drive, Coach Mack called our new trick play—Wide Receiver Left/Reverse/Option Pass.

It worked great. I handed the ball to Devro on a reverse. The Bullis defense fell for the fake and came charging after him. This gave Luke a chance to slip behind the Bullis defensive backs. Devro got the pass off just before the Bullis guys tackled him. The ball was a little wobbly but right on the money. Luke hauled it in at the 40-yard line and raced the length of the field for the touchdown.

We made the 2-point conversion on a pass to Devro. We were ahead, 8–0.

Everyone on the sidelines was pumped. "Maybe we should run nothing but trick plays," I said to Brandon and Michelle.

Bullis came right back. They drove down the field using running plays that ate up yardage and the clock. It seemed like our offense had been on the sidelines for an hour when Bullis finally crashed over from the two-yard line for a score. They missed the extra point, though, so we were still ahead, 8–6.

We couldn't move the ball and were forced to punt. The Bullis offense pounded out another long drive that ended in another touchdown.

We were behind 14–8 at halftime. Coach Mack gave us another pep talk. "We're still in it," he said. "We've just got to keep playing hard."

Bullis kicked off to start the second half.

Devro caught the ball at the ten-yard line, sprinted straight up the middle, broke a couple of tackles, then at the 25 he bolted left and took off down the sideline.

He was gone. *Touchdown!* I hit Devro on a quick Down and Out and we were ahead, 16–14. We were all jumping up and down, celebrating, and, for a second, I was thinking, hey, maybe we can beat these guys.

But it was all Bullis after that. They stopped us cold. We tried that other trick play—Flare Right/Quarterback Pass Back— where Devro lines up at quarterback and throws a pass back to me at wide receiver, then goes out for a pass. The play didn't fool anybody. A Bullis tackler hit me just as I threw the ball. It landed 20 yards short of Devro.

The Bullis offense put together some long scoring drives just the way they did in the first half. We lost 30–16. Not too bad. At least it was closer than last time.

So there were no last-play heroics like in *Instant Replay*. I guess I need to work on my happy endings.

Michelle handed me the game stats as we rode back on the bus. I looked them over for a few seconds. There was no need to study them. Bullis was just better than we were.

"Do you want the season statistics?" she asked.

"Sure. Might as well add them to my journal."

SEASON LEADERS

PASSING:	C/ATTS	YARDS	TDS	INTS
MONROE:	80/139	1073	13	7
BEECH:	15/30	199	1	0
RUSHING:	ATTS	YARDS	TDS	
JENKINS:	132	516	5	
BEECH:	31	198	0	
RECEIVING:	RECS	YARDS	TDS	
GONZALEZ:	33	437	5	
BEECH:	21	427	6	
CONSTANTINO:	25	216	3	

"You're still keeping that journal? I thought your English assignment was over."

"It is," I said, wishing I hadn't brought it up. "But it's fun to have a record of the entire football season."

"Yeah, that'll be cool," she agreed. "Are you going to the sports awards banquet tomorrow night?"

"Yeah, Coach Mack says we have to go."

Michelle smiled. "Maybe you'll get an award for best sportswriter."

Friday, November 19

The sports award banquet was held in the Parkside cafeteria. Even on a Friday night the place still smelled like sloppy joes and french fries. All the fall sports teams—boys soccer, girls soccer, field hockey, football—sat together. It was funny to see Michelle sitting there in the middle of fifty guys. The parents' tables were at the back of the cafeteria.

Coach Mack is strict about the sports banquet. He makes every guy on the team dress and act nicely—no jeans, no T-shirts, no fooling around.

Each coach gives out three awards: Most Valuable Player, the top award; Most Improved Player; and the Coach's Award, for the kid who helps the team the most without necessarily being a great player.

Coach Mack gave out his awards last. He congratulated us on a very good season and said he was proud of each member of the team. Coach also thanked Mr. Shortall for all his help.

He gave Most Improved Player to Brady Terres. That was cool. Brady was the one who stepped in when Dan Jankowski quit. He did a great job in the offensive line.

The second award was a bit of a surprise. "My Coach's Award," he said, "goes to someone who never played a single minute during the season, but helped the team in so many ways: our manager, Michelle Campano."

All the guys gave Michelle a standing ovation. Her face turned as red as a tomato. We whistled and cheered loudly until Coach gave a signal for us to sit down. He was right to give her that award. Michelle kept the stats, helped Colby with his math, and did a zillion other things that helped the team.

Then Coach Mack began talking again. "My MVP did a little of everything this season. He led us in scoring, returned kicks, and played some quarterback..."

I couldn't believe it. *Devro was going to be MVP?* I could barely listen as Coach Mack went through all the things Devro had done. It was all true, but he was a seventh grader! Why couldn't Coach have waited until next year to give him the MVP?

By the time I started listening again, Coach didn't seem to be talking about Devro anymore.

"...he led our team in passing, touchdown passes, and helped us win six games this season. And you can't win games unless you have a good, steady quarterback."

Coach Mack scooped up two trophies from the table. "So I have *two* Most Valuable Players this season," he said. "Devro Beech and Matt Monroe."

I barely heard Coach call my name.

Brandon and Colby and the other guys (even Michelle) were slapping me on the back and cheering.

I looked back at my parents as I walked toward Coach Mack. They were smiling and clapping. Devro and I fell in beside each other. Devro reached out his fist and we shared a quick fist bump. I shook hands with Coach Mack, thanked him, took the trophy, and headed back to my seat.

I know it's not an NFL championship or a Super Bowl, but I think getting the MVP trophy—and sharing it with Devro—is a pretty good happy ending.

Monday, November 22

This morning, Mr. Harris, a science teacher and the school's track coach, saw me in the corridor and asked me whether I wanted to run in the winter track program. "It would be a great way for you to stay in shape," he said.

"I'm not that fast," I said.

"That's okay," he said. "You can run middle distances like the 800 and the 1600 meter runs. I can help you get faster."

"You should get Devro to run for you," I said. "He's super fast."

"He's playing basketball," Mr. Harris said. "What do you say? Do you want to run track?"

I told him I'd think about it.

I didn't go home right away after school. It seemed like forever since I'd been home while it was light outside. I walked up to the football field. Nobody was there, just some lady throwing a tennis ball with her golden retriever. The dog never got tired of chasing the ball and bringing it back.

Dogs are kind of like linemen—they think the stupidest things are fun.

I sat in the stands. A cold wind whipped across the open field. I plunged my hands into my coat pockets to keep them warm. I thought about the football season that had just ended. Winning the MVP award will help me when I try out for the Whitman team next year.

Then I thought about what Mr. Harris had said. Winter track would give me something to do after school and it would keep me in shape for other sports, especially football.

I like being part of a team.

And I can write about winter track.

The Real Story

It's not surprising that Pop-Pop—Matt's grandfather—had a copy of the book, *Instant Replay*. Published in 1968, *Instant Replay* was on the *New York Times* best-seller list for thirty-seven weeks.

The book was one of the first inside looks at what it was like to be a professional football player. Remember, the book was published before ESPN and 24-hour-a-day sports television coverage. In the late sixties, pro football was just beginning to gain wide popularity.

Two very different men worked together as a team to make the book a big success. Dick Schaap was a magazine and newspaper sportswriter and columnist. Jerry Kramer was a five-time All-Pro offensive guard for the Green Bay Packers.

Schaap met Kramer while writing a magazine article on Kramer's teammate and training camp roommate, Packers rugged fullback Jim Taylor. The sportswriter first encountered Kramer in their dorm room doing something that seemed unusual for a big, tough football player—he was reading poetry out loud. So years later when a book publisher asked Schaap if he knew a pro football player who might keep a diary about his season, Schaap immediately thought of Kramer.

As Matt mentioned in *Quarterback Season*, Kramer kept the diary by speaking into a tape recorder a few times a week. He then sent the tapes to Schaap, who would "organize, condense, clarify, and punctuate" Kramer's words. Schaap was very clear that he did not write the book. As he said in the introduction to *Instant Replay*, "If anyone suspects that I placed words in Jerry Kramer's mouth, he credits me with too much courage. I would never put words in the mouth of anyone three inches taller and sixty-five pounds heavier than I."

The stories in *Instant Replay* are Kramer's, and he told lots of them about a variety of topics:

• Contract negotiations. Kramer was paid only $27,500 for the 1967 season. Today, All-Pro players make millions of dollars.

• The physically demanding nature of pro football, especially the two-a-day practices in training camp. Like Matt, Kramer hated certain drills.

• Players who would sometimes sneak out of training camp at night, even though it was against the rules.

• Players' fears that they would be cut from the team during training camp.

• Injuries and playing with pain.

• The challenge that teammates with different personalities and from different races, religions, and backgrounds faced as they tried to work together.

- The games: the wins and losses and the ups and downs of the season.

But most of all, Kramer told stories about the Packers' legendary coach, Vince Lombardi. Kramer describes Lombardi as tough and hard-driving. The Packers had won the first Super Bowl the year before, but Lombardi would not allow the players to become satisfied or lazy. He worked them harder than any team in the NFL. Lombardi said, "The harder a man works, the harder it is for him to surrender."

Kramer also revealed that Coach Lombardi had a genius for figuring out how to motivate his players to play their best. Just when Kramer was sick of Lombardi's screaming and constant criticism, Lombardi would put his arm around Kramer and tell him how good a player he was and how much he meant to the team. Gestures like this from his coach made Kramer want to play even harder.

There is no doubt that Lombardi was a great coach. After all, the trophy for the winner of the Super Bowl is named the Lombardi Trophy.

Lombardi was born in New York City in 1913. He attended Fordham University on a football scholarship. At the time, the Fordham Rams had one of the best football teams in the country. Even though Lombardi was not big (5 feet 8 inches tall and 180 pounds), he played in the offensive line. The Rams offensive line was terrific. They were known as "The Seven Blocks of Granite."

After college, Lombardi coached football and taught Latin, chemistry, and physics at St. Cecilia's, a Catholic high school in New Jersey. After several years at St. Cecilia's, Lombardi landed an assistant coaching job at West Point, the United States Military Academy.

Lombardi began his pro coaching career when he became an assistant coach and the offensive coordinator with the New York Giants in 1954. The Giants did very well with Lombardi designing the plays. They defeated the Chicago Bears, 47–7, for the NFL championship in 1956.

In 1959, Lombardi became the head coach of the Green Bay Packers. At that time the Packers were the worst team in pro football. The year before Lombardi arrived in Green Bay, the Packers had a record of 1–10–1 (one win, ten losses, and one tie). They hadn't had a winning record in eleven consecutive seasons.

Lombardi transformed the Packers into winners. The Packers and Lombardi never had a losing record during his nine seasons as head coach at Green Bay. The Packers won three NFL titles (1961, 1962, and 1965) as well as the first two Super Bowls ever played. Green Bay won so often that football fans started calling the city "Titletown, U.S.A."

The 1967 season that Kramer wrote about in *Instant Replay* was Lombardi's last with Green Bay. The Packers had a regular season record of 9–4–1. They beat the Los Angeles Rams in the first round of the NFL playoffs, 28–7, and then defeated the Dallas Cowboys for the NFL title.

As Matt describes in his journal, the 1967 game between the Packers and the Cowboys was one of the most famous games in the history of professional football. The temperature in Green Bay at game time was an unbelievable 13 degrees below zero!

That year the Packers went on to beat the Oakland Raiders, 33–14, in Super Bowl II. So Lombardi left Green Bay a winner.

Many famous athletes and coaches have written books describing their teams and the games they play, but like Pop-Pop says, *Instant Replay* is still one of the best sports books around.

About the Author

Fred Bowen was a Little Leaguer who loved to read. Now he is the author of many action-packed books of sports fiction. He has also written a weekly sports column for kids in *The Washington Post* since 2000.

For thirteen years, Fred coached kids' baseball and basketball teams. Some of his stories spring directly from his coaching experience and his sports-happy childhood in Massachusetts.

Fred holds a degree in history from the University of Pennsylvania and a law degree from George Washington University. He was a lawyer for many years before retiring to become a full-time children's author. Bowen has been a guest author at schools and conferences across the country, as well as the Smithsonian Institute in Washington, DC, and The Baseball Hall of Fame.

Fred lives in Silver Spring, Maryland, with his wife Peggy Jackson. Their son is a college baseball coach and their daughter is a college student.

Be sure to check out the author's websites.
www.fredbowen.com
www.SportsStorySeries.com

Become a fan of Fred Bowen on Facebook!

HEY, SPORTS FANS!

Don't miss these action-packed books by Fred Bowen...

Want more?

All-Star Sports Story
Series

T. J.'s Secret Pitch
PB: $5.95 / 978-1-56145-504-1 / 1-56145-504-0

T. J.'s pitches just don't pack the power to strike out the batters, but the story of 1940s baseball hero Rip Sewell and his legendary eephus pitch may help him find a solution.

The Golden Glove
PB: $5.95 / 978-1-56145-505-8 / 1-56145-505-9

Without his lucky glove, Jamie doesn't believe in his ability to lead his baseball team to victory. How will he learn that faith in oneself is the most important equipment for any game?

The Kid Coach
PB: $5.95 / 978-1-56145-506-5 / 1-56145-506-7

Scott and his teammates can't find an adult to coach their team, so they must find a leader among themselves.

Playoff Dreams
PB: $5.95 / 978-1-56145-507-2 / 1-56145-507-5

Brendan is one of the best players in the league, but no matter how hard he tries, he can't make his team win.

Winners Take All
PB: $5.95 / 978-1-56145-512-6 / 1-56145-512-1

Kyle makes a poor decision to cheat in a big game. Someone discovers the truth and threatens to reveal it. What can Kyle do now?

All-Star Sports Story series